Dear Parent:
Your child's love of reading starts here!

Every child learns to read in a different way and at his or her own speed. Some go back and forth between reading levels and read favorite books again and again. Others read through each level in order. You can help your young reader improve and become more confident by encouraging his or her own interests and abilities. From books your child reads with you to the first books he or she reads alone, there are I Can Read Books for every stage of reading:

SHARED READING
Basic language, word repetition, and whimsical illustrations, ideal for sharing with your emergent reader

BEGINNING READING
Short sentences, familiar words, and simple concepts for children eager to read on their own

READING WITH HELP
Engaging stories, longer sentences, and language play for developing readers

READING ALONE
Complex plots, challenging vocabulary, and high-interest topics for the independent reader

I Can Read Books have introduced children to the joy of reading since 1957. Featuring award-winning authors and illustrators and a fabulous cast of beloved characters, I Can Read Books set the standard for beginning readers.

A lifetime of discovery begins with the magical words "I Can Read!"

Visit www.icanread.com for information
on enriching your child's reading experience.

Magic Mixies: Castle Quest!
Copyright © 2023 The Moose Group. MAGIC MIXIES MIXLINGS™ logos, names,
and characters are licensed trademarks of Moose Enterprises (INT) Pty Ltd.
All rights reserved. Printed in the United States of America.
No part of this book may be used or reproduced in any manner whatsoever without written permission
except in the case of brief quotations embodied in critical articles and reviews.
For information address HarperCollins Children's Books, a division of HarperCollins Publishers,
195 Broadway, New York, NY 10007.
www.icanread.com

Library of Congress Control Number: 2023933921
ISBN 978-0-06-331093-3

23 24 25 26 27 LB 10 9 8 7 6 5 4 3 2 1
First Edition

I Can Read!

Castle Quest!

Adapted by Mickey Domenici
Based on the episodes
"The Highest Tower" & "Magicus Mixus!"
written by Katie Chilson

HARPER
An Imprint of HarperCollinsPublishers

After going through a portal,

Sienna is stuck in Mixia!

Mixia is a world full of magic.

The Mixlings are helping

Sienna get home.

Mixlings are magical creatures.
Geckler, Parlo, Dawne, Luggle,
Pixly, and Carrot are all excited
to help Sienna.

Sienna loves her new friends,
but she must return home
for her lolo's birthday party.
Lolo means grandpa.

The castle is the only place with
strong enough magic to get her home.
With her friends' help,
Sienna finally arrives at the castle!

The Castle sparkles with crystals,
but it's tiny!

They can't even fit through the door!

Sienna casts a spell.

Suddenly, the Castle widens!

The tower shoots into the sky.

The crystal over the door glows.

Everyone can't wait to go inside.

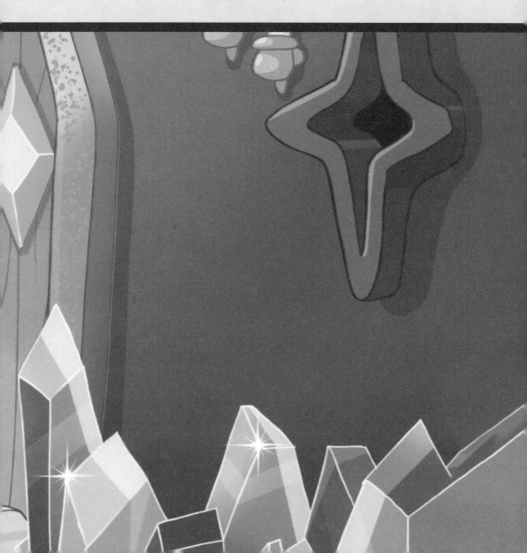

The main hall glitters with gems.

Carrot says they need to find

the highest tower.

It's where the magic is strongest.

Suddenly the friends realize

they are about to lose Sienna forever.

They don't want her to go home.

The friends decide to use
the Castle's magic
to make Sienna stay!

First, Carrot discovers that
the Castle's magic has created a feast.
So the friends start a food fight!

Then Dawne tries to make
Sienna take a nap.
Next, Geckler says he wants
to throw a goodbye party.

But Sienna keeps making her way
toward the tower.

Suddenly, the stairs become a ramp
and Sienna falls.

It's the Castle's magic!

Sienna runs away to a closet.
She realizes that her friends
don't want her to leave.
But she needs to get home.

With her wand, she turns an old bucket
into a cauldron and casts a spell.

"Magicus Mixus!"

She will summon a new Mixling
if no one else will help.

17

This Mixling is named Zarla.

Zarla leads Sienna to the tower.

Sienna is casting a spell

when Carrot and the others arrive.

But the spell doesn't work.

It creates a magic tornado

that sucks up all the Mixlings!

Then a Mixling wearing

a suit of armor appears!

The strange Mixling flutters its wings

and breaks up the storm.

The Mixlings are safe!

Everyone shares a big hug.

21

"We're sorry for tricking you,"

says Luggle.

"But you helped us anyway!" says Pixly.

"You're a really good friend."

The Mixling in the armor is Magique,
the Castle's caretaker.
Magique warns them that
the Castle's magic is too strong!

Sienna needs her friends' help
to control the Castle's magic.
She stands tall with her friends
and speaks from her heart.

"I will gather my love in the Tower,

because alone my magic

doesn't hold enough power.

To finally bring this to an end,

I must rely on my Mixia friends."

MAGICUS MIXUS!

The magic
becomes
a dragon!

Pixly charms
the dragon
with her magic.

Geckler and Zarla
glow extra bright!

Then Sienna blasts it away!
The long fight to control
the Castle's magic is over.

Sienna casts one more spell
to fix the Castle.

It's time for Sienna to go home.

The Mixlings each say goodbye.

Yay, Sienna is finally home!
She made it just in time
for her lolo's birthday party.

She will miss her friends,
but for now she is happy
to be home.

Magicus Mixus!

Magic ingredients are hidden in the pages.

Can you find them all?